W9-BXX-954

Chicks and Salsa

BY

Aaron Reynolds

ILLUSTRATED BY

Paulette Bogan

BLOOMSBURY
NEW YORK LONDON OXFORD NEW DELHI SYDNEY

Text copyright © 2005 by Aaron Reynolds
Illustrations copyright © 2005 by Paulette Bogan
All rights reserved. No part of this book may be reproduced or transmitted in any form
or by any means, electronic or mechanical, including photocopying, recording, or by any
information storage and retrieval system, without permission in writing from the publisher.

First published in the United States of America in October 2005
by Bloomsbury Children's Books
Paperback edition published in May 2007
www.bloomsbury.com

Bloomsbury is a registered trademark of Bloomsbury Publishing Plc

For information about permission to reproduce selections from this book, write to
Permissions, Bloomsbury Children's Books, 1385 Broadway, New York, New York 10018
Bloomsbury books may be purchased for business or promotional use. For information on bulk purchases
please contact Macmillan Corporate and Premium Sales Department at specialmarkets@macmillan.com

The Library of Congress has cataloged the hardcover edition as follows:
Reynolds, Aaron.
Chicks and salsa / by Aaron Reynolds ; illustrated by Paulette Bogan. — 1st U.S. ed.
p.   cm.
Summary: Soon after the chickens tire of their feed and decide to make tortilla chips and salsa,
all the other animals on Nuthatcher Farm start to crave southwestern cuisine.
ISBN-13: 978-1-58234-972-5 · ISBN-10: 1-58234-972-X (hardcover)
[1. Chickens—Fiction. 2. Domestic animals—Fiction. 3. Cookery—Fiction. 4. Farms—Fiction.]
I. Bogan, Paulette, ill. II. Title.
PZ7.R33213Ch2005   [E]—dc22   2005042137

ISBN-13: 978-1-59990-099-5 · ISBN-10: 1-59990-099-8 (paperback)

Typeset in Circus Mouse Book
Art created with watercolor
Design by Marikka Tamura

Printed in China by RR Donnelley
20 19 18 17 16 15 14

All papers used by Bloomsbury Publishing, Inc., are natural, recyclable products
made from wood grown in well-managed forests. The manufacturing
processes conform to the environmental regulations of the
country of origin.

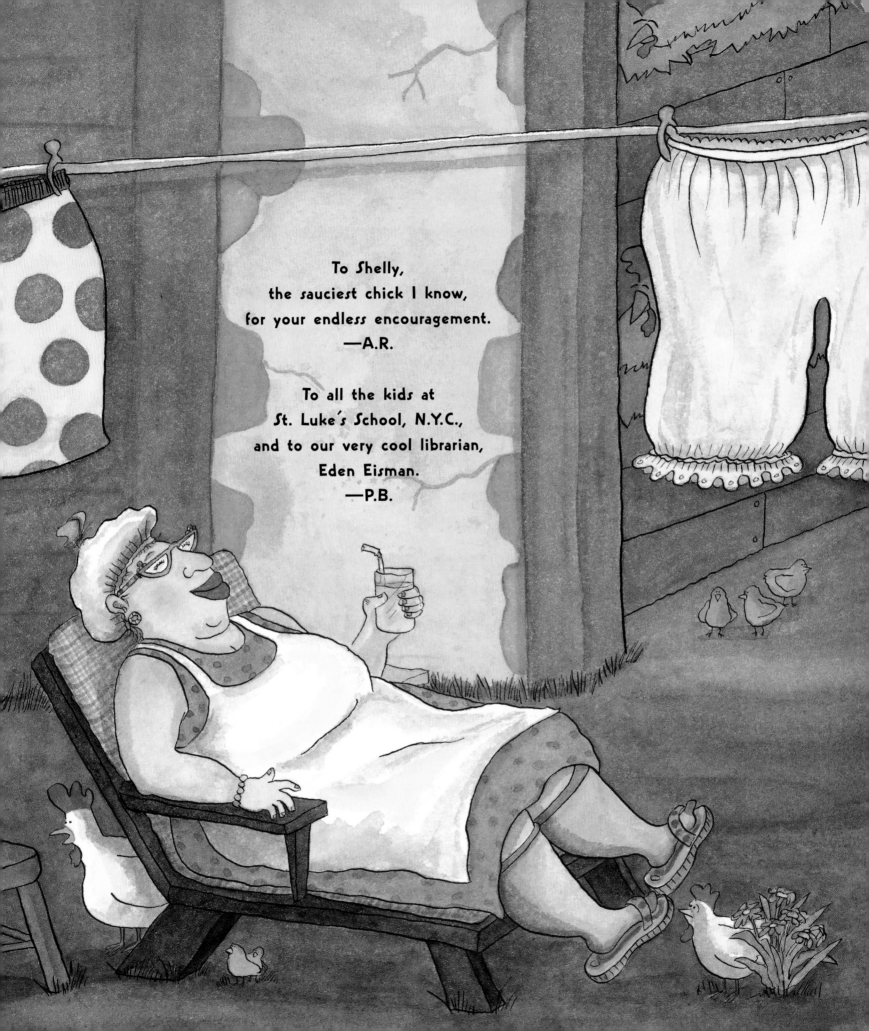

To Shelly,
the sauciest chick I know,
for your endless encouragement.
—A.R.

To all the kids at
St. Luke's School, N.Y.C.,
and to our very cool librarian,
Eden Eisman.
—P.B.

There were grumblings in the henhouse of Nuthatcher
Farm. The chickens were tired of chicken feed.
The rooster took it upon himself to solve this problem.

Mrs. Nuthatcher, the farmer's wife, had started watching cooking shows in the afternoons. The rooster was perched on a fence post outside the farmhouse window when he discovered the solution to his problem . . .

Led by the rooster, the chickens crept into the garden,
where they took tomatoes and uprooted onions.

That night, the chickens ate chips and salsa—
though nobody was quite certain where
the chickens got the chips.

The tasty tang of tomatoes and onions hung
over the barnyard.
And the rooster said, **"Olé!"**

Very soon, there were mumblings at the duck pond of
Nuthatcher Farm. Inspired by the chickens, the ducks
decided they were tired of fish.

With the rooster's encouragement, the ducks dipped
into the garden, where they selected cilantro
and gathered garlic.

That night the ducks ate guacamole—though nobody was quite certain where the ducks got the avocados.

The spicy scent of garlic and cilantro
hung over the barnyard.
And the ducks said, "Olé!"

The next morning, there were rumblings in the pigpen of Nuthatcher Farm. Overwhelmed by the enticing aromas, the pigs decided they were tired of slop.

While the rooster distracted Farmer Nuthatcher,
the pigs plodded into the garden, where they
borrowed beans and chopped chiles.

That night, the pigs ate nachos—though nobody was quite certain where the pigs got the nacho cheese sauce.

The delightful deliciousness of cheese and chiles hung over the barnyard.

And the pigs said, "Olé!"

As everyone knows, when a passion for southwestern cuisine takes hold of farm animals, and so many sumptuous, spicy, savory scents collide in the barnyard air, it can only lead to one thing . . .

FIESTA!

The rooster got things organized, then returned to his fence post to watch for a good enchilada recipe. The horses decorated the barn.

The bull practiced his Mexican hat dance—though nobody was quite certain where the bull got the sombrero.

And the chickens, ducks, and pigs snuck into the garden.
But all of their spicy southwestern supplies were gone!

The scallions had been stolen!
The peppers had been pilfered!
The limes had been lifted!

But there were slurpings in the kitchen of Nuthatcher Farm. Stirred by the succulent smells in the barnyard, Mrs. Nuthatcher had decided to make tamales for the county fair.

A saucy sweetness hung over the farmhouse kitchen.
And Mrs. Nuthatcher said, "Olé!"

Disappointed, the animals canceled the fiesta.

That evening the chickens ate their chicken feed,
the ducks ate their fish, and the pigs ate their slop.

But while the Nuthatchers were at the fair, the rooster crept into the kitchen and borrowed a French cookbook. The next morning, the rooster ate crêpes with white grapes in champagne sauce.

Though nobody was quite certain where the rooster learned how to read.

A satisfied smile stretched over the rooster's beak.
And the rooster said, "Ooh la la!"